SOMETHING DIFFERENT ABOUT DAD

How to Live with Your Amazing Asperger Parent

Kirsti Evans and John Swogger

JKP

Jessica Kingsley *Publishers*
London and Philadelphia

This second edition published in 2016
by Jessica Kingsley Publishers
73 Collier Street
London N1 9BE, UK
and
400 Market Street, Suite 400
Philadelphia, PA 19106, USA

www.jkp.com

First edition published by Jessica Kingsley Publishers, 2010

Library of Congress Cataloging in Publication Data
A CIP catalog record for this book is available from the Library of Congress

British Library Cataloguing in Publication Data
A CIP catalogue record for this book is available from the British Library

ISBN 978 1 78592 012 7
eISBN 978 1 78450 259 1

Printed and bound in Great Britain

For Rosie and Sonny

Preface

The original edition of this book, which came out in 2011, was intended for children and young people who knew and/or were living with an adult on the Autism Spectrum, whether formally diagnosed or not.

Since then, not only have there been even further increases in the number of diagnoses in adults, there have also been many developments in our general awareness and recognition of Autism socially and culturally, not least in the increased recognition of women and girls who have Autism and Asperger Syndrome.

Things have also developed with regards to how we think and talk about Autism: what we call it, how we see it.

The fifth, most recent, edition of the American publication *The Diagnostic and Statistical Manual of Mental Disorders* doesn't employ the name "Asperger Syndrome" as a description of a condition separate from "Autistic Spectrum Disorder". Instead, Asperger Syndrome is now incorporated into the broader classification of Autism Spectrum Disorder. This has led to some differences of opinion as to whether people who have previously been identified as having Asperger Syndrome should now be termed simply "Autistic".

We are aware that a great many people in the world firmly see themselves as having Asperger Syndrome and much prefer to use that term to identify themselves and to describe their individual life experiences. Much discussion has taken place on this matter, with some people worrying that their original diagnosis of Asperger Syndrome is no longer valid and won't be recognised as such. This is, of course, not the case. The global Aspergers community is alive and well – lots and lots of people continue to use the term to describe what is an integral part of who they are.

We have chosen to continue with our use of the term "Asperger Syndrome" in *Something Different About Dad*, as we feel this currently reflects the views and experiences of all you amazing people out there.

Kirsti Evans and John Swogger
April 2016

Contents

Introduction

Hello! My name is **Kirsti** and I work with children and adults who have Autism and Asperger Syndrome. I wrote this book...

And this is **John**, who works as a book and magazine illustrator. He helped me tell the story by drawing all the pictures.

Hi!

This book is for anyone who has an adult relative with Asperger Syndrome.

It might be a parent...

...or grandparent...

...an uncle, or aunt...

...or even an older brother or sister.

This book follows the story of **Sophie**...

...whose Dad, **Mark**, has Asperger Syndrome.

Perhaps, like Sophie, you may not have noticed that your relative was "different" when you were younger...

...but maybe now you are starting to see that there is "something different" about them.

Whether or not you know for sure that the person you are thinking of is the same as Sophie's dad...

...we hope reading Sophie's story will help answer some of the questions you might have...

...and make it easier for you understand the adults with Asperger Syndrome in your life.

Kirsti + John

1. This Is My Family

The story I'm going to tell you will be about some of the problems we had with some of the things Dad would do or say.

It's a story about how sometimes living with Dad was difficult and frustrating...

...and about how sometimes Dad makes us upset and angry.

But it's also a story about us starting to understand Dad better...

...and understand that there are things we can do to make living with Dad less difficult and less frustrating.

And it's a story about us realising that we don't love Dad any <u>less</u> because he has Asperger Syndrome!

I still love my Dad and I think he's the best Dad in the world...

...<u>because</u> he's different!

This is a story about my dad - but it's a story about all the people who know him, too - people at work, people in shops, my teachers at school, friends, neighbours...

It's also a story about us, his family: my mum Vicky, my brother Daniel, my Uncle Jason and Auntie Louise, my cousins Lilly and Barney (and their dog, Buster!) and my Grandpa Fred.

This is a photo of us at Haven Parcs last summer, where we all went on holiday - it was so cool!

I really, really hope we get to go back there again this year...

This is all of us - me in the front, Daniel next to me and Grandpa Fred behind him. Auntie Louise is behind me, carrying Lilly, and Uncle Jason is in the back, with Barney on his shoulders. And that's Mum and Dad next to them.

And look! I got to hold Buster!

We all went on holiday together last summer.

It was so much fun!

Everyone had a GREAT time...

Well...maybe not Dad...

...FF TO INCREASE AT HOSPITAL

...AHEAD GIVEN TO NEW SUPPORT AND PATIENT EDUCATION TEAMS

...en new support workers join nurses and surgeons at the County clinic ...he most recent round of expansion for the new Trust. The move has been ...oadly welcomed by patient groups, including Hip and Knee Joint School. ...ut questions still remain over long-term funding for the extra jobs.

Support worker Vicky at County Trust Hospital, yesterday.

But I had a really, really great time – and I really, really, really want to go back again this summer. Mum says she and Dad have to "discuss it".

I hope Dad says yes...

That's my mum – in the newspaper! She's the coolest! She works in the hospital – the big one up by the roundabout. She helps nurses look after people.

So does her friend Lucy. She has a grumpy old cat called Malcolm, and really, really likes anything Spanish. She and Mum used to do loads of things together – like go to dance classes at the community centre.

Mum tried to get Dad to go – but he hated it!

There's only one thing Dad likes...

...and that's BUSES!

Dad is an inspector at the Bus Depot. He checks all the buses to make sure they're safe.

Dad LOVES buses...

...so he really, really loves his job!

He's always on time for work – and never, ever takes a day off unless Mum makes him!

And all he thinks about is buses – all day long...

...and not just at work, either.

At home he's got loads of bus books and magazines in the front room – and loads of bus models as well.

Dad keeps them really tidy.

I mean _really_ tidy.

Dad likes everything to be really tidy anyway. I'm okay, I suppose, but my brother Daniel is really messy.

Dad shouts at him all the time to clean up his room and stop making so much noise.

Daniel makes a <u>lot</u> of noise.

Daniel really, <u>really</u> likes football. He's <u>dead</u> good at it.

Dad <u>doesn't</u> like football. It's too noisy.

So instead, Daniel plays with Uncle Jason. Uncle Jase loves football almost as much as Daniel does! They support Town F.C. (I think) and go to real football games at the big grounds. They always have a great time - and get to make as much noise as they want!

Uncle Jase is married to Auntie Louise, and they're both really cool!

They're always laughing and telling jokes.

They love the seaside. Mum told me they even got married on the beach!

They've got two kids...

...my cousins, Lilly and Barney. Louise calls them "little monkeys".

They've also got a dog, Buster. I think Buster's great!

Dad doesn't like Buster...

Uncle Jason and Auntie Louise live really close by. Lots of people we know live close to us – like Mrs. Chang, our neighbour (who loves to talk!).

She cooks really amazing food and invites us over sometimes. Daniel and I love her dumplings...

I don't know if Dad does though...

Grandpa Fred lives near us, too.

He's Dad and Uncle Jase's dad.

Any more fares, please!

He used to be a bus conductor, and knows loads of stories about working on the old buses.

Who else can I tell you about?

oh yeah...

ME!

I like school - I've got a great teacher, Ms. Farmer, and I love doing art.

She always tells me how good my drawings are and puts them up on the wall in the classroom. I can't wait to show Mum and Dad when they come to school for the Parents' Evening.

What else?

Well, obviously, I like writing in my journal!

I also really, really like karaoke. I've got all the DVDs for the "My School Musical" song set, and loads and loads of other stuff - like stickers and magazines and things.

Daniel says its stupid, but I like the songs. A lot of them are about friends and your family - and I like that.

And I <u>love</u> Haven Parcs. I really, really hope we get to go back there again this summer...

Hey – I'd better go. It's almost 6:15, and Dad always has tea <u>exactly</u> at 6:15 – I mean, <u>exactly</u>. He gets really mad if Daniel stays out playing football and makes tea late.

Maybe you can see what I mean about my dad – there's just something a bit...<u>different</u> about him.

Maybe I'm only noticing it now 'cause I'm a bit older. I mean, it's not <u>loads</u> of things – and not, like, <u>loads</u> different. But...well...

But you'll see what I mean. I'll show you what he was like at the Parents' Evening, and I'll show you what he was like when we tried to talk about next summer's holiday.

I think then you'll understand exactly what kind of "different" I'm talking about.

So what kind of "different" is Sophie talking about?

She's told us a little bit about her family, and about her dad.

I think I can see what she's talking about – her dad is very interested in buses, likes to have set times for things and seems to get upset when things aren't as he would have liked them or are unexpected.

Sophie says that she's maybe noticing that her dad is different because she's getting a little older. Both she and her brother Daniel are starting to grow up and change a bit themselves.

Sophie has told us that her dad has <u>Asperger Syndrome</u>.

But before we let Sophie tell us any more about her and her family, perhaps we'd better answer an important question...

2. So What Is Asperger Syndrome?

Asperger Syndrome is named after the Doctor who first discovered it: Hans Asperger.

Sometimes it's also called Asperger's Syndrome, and sometimes it's shortened to AS.

It's also referred to as part of the Autism Spectrum, and you might hear it called Autism Spectrum Disorder – sometimes shortened to ASD.

A lot of people are still not sure what to call it, since it can be difficult to tell if someone's behaviour is a result of AS or something else.

We'll be using the terms Asperger Syndrome and AS in this book, but whatever name you give it, it's about behaving differently –

but behaving differently in a very particular way.

Lots of people can have Asperger Syndrome...

Some of them will know about it...

...and some of them won't.

Some people find out they have it when they're young – and some people, like Sophie's dad, don't find out about it until they're grown up.

These days, more people know about AS than in the past, especially people who work with children, like doctors and school teachers...

...so it's more common now for people to find out about it when they're younger and in school.

When Mark was growing up, not that many people knew about AS...

But if he was a kid today, someone would probably notice he was a bit...

...different.

1976 Birthday

Birthday 1979

Birthday! 1984

New Job! 1992

People with Asperger Syndrome don't <u>look</u> different to anyone else – they have jobs and families like other people.

But they do <u>behave</u> differently...

Although everyone who has AS is affected by it in their own way, they share similar <u>difficulties</u>, <u>differences</u> and <u>talents</u>. This means that AS can make someone talk and act differently to how you might usually expect.

We've grouped all these difficulties, differences and talents into four main areas:

IMAGINATION

one way to do things

schedules and timetables

special interests

special talents

liking to know what happens when

routine

knowing in advance

liking things
to be the same

fascination with
detail

lack of flexibility

COMMUNICATION

taking things literally

not understanding other people

taking time to "process"

difficulty making friends

struggling
with conversation

not understanding
jokes

things
too loud!

too much going on

difficulty sleeping

difficulty relaxing

seeming odd
or weird

seeming rude
or stupid

wanting to be alone

THE SENSES

EMOTIONS &
RELATIONSHIPS

27

Throughout the rest of this book we'll be looking at how AS difficulties, differences and talents in each of these four areas can affect everyday situations.

We'll also see how all these areas are connected – how difficulties with <u>imagination</u>, for example, are linked to difficulties with <u>communication</u>, or how difficulties with <u>emotions and relationships</u> can be linked to difficulties with the <u>senses</u>.

And, by listening to Sophie's story about Mark and her family, we'll see how people with AS and their families can help manage difficult situations as they understand more about Asperger Syndrome.

Let's look at each of these four main areas in turn, starting with:

Dad! Buster chewed up my favourite football!

That's why I don't like dogs.

EMOTIONS & RELATIONSHIPS

When we look at this area of AS, we'll see how it makes it hard for Mark to understand how other people are feeling. Sometimes, people with AS have difficulty "reading" someone else's reaction to something or understanding things like facial expressions, which would give them a clue about how another person feels.

Sometimes they might have difficulty showing their <u>own</u> feelings. This can make them behave in ways that can seem odd or strange to people who don't know them very well.

If you're not happy with it, sir, we can offer you an alternative...

It's fine.

It's no trouble!

It's fine.

They can end up seeming like they don't care about people, and can sometimes make people they care about very upset.

We'll see how this part of Mark's AS affects Sophie and the rest of the family.

COMMUNICATION

Many people with AS are very good at talking – as long as it's something <u>they</u> like talking about.

But they may not be very good at holding a <u>conversation.</u>

We'll see that Mark has difficulty sometimes understanding what people are saying to him. He occasionally needs time to understand – or "process" – information.

oh, I know – the way Mark goes <u>on</u> and <u>on</u> about buses!

We'll talk more about this and what we call "special interests" a bit later on.

It can be hard for people around Mark to realise that he needs this extra time.

And this can become a problem when there are lots of people around and lots of different conversations happening at the same time.

We'll see an example of how this affects Mark in Chapter 3.

IMAGINATION

This is all about how people put together information in their own heads. People use their imagination to understand that things <u>might</u> or <u>could</u> happen.

People with AS often have difficulty with this kind of thinking, and are most comfortable when they know exactly <u>what</u> is going to happen and <u>when</u> it's going to happen.

People with AS tend to like routines, and can find sudden changes of plan confusing.

Mark is like this – he likes to do certain things at certain times.

And we'll see how he finds it difficult to cope when things happen that he didn't have time to think about beforehand.

We'll see some examples of this in Chapter 3 and Chapter 4.

Imagination is important for understanding another person's point of view – this is called "empathy".

Imagination helps people see things from a different angle, and helps people to see that there might be more than one way to understand things.

Imagination is very important when we say things that shouldn't be taken literally – sayings and expressions like "Put yourself in my shoes" or "It's raining cats and dogs".

Misunderstandings with language because of difficulties with imagination can sometimes make conversations extra difficult for people with AS.

This is an example of the way in which difficulties in one area can be connected to difficulties in another area.

THE SENSES

Hearing, sight, taste, touch and smell - these are our senses. They are how we find out about the world. How we react to what we hear, what we see, what we taste and what we smell is very important to us.

Think about how people have favourite colours or favourite foods, for example.

But people with AS can find it hard to cope with some sorts of noises, some kinds of light or certain smells.

People with AS can find lots of different noises together really confusing - being in a room with lots of people all talking at once, for example. Or they can find really bright lights uncomfortable, or they may find particular smells or textures really unpleasant or distracting.

Some people with AS even find that their sense of balance, or sense of space - their sense of what is around them - is different.

All this can make people with AS seem fussy, spoiled, irritable or clumsy to other people - but it's just a different reaction to "sensory" information.

We'll talk a bit more about how sensory issues affect Mark in Chapter 4.

SPECIAL INTERESTS

Most people with AS have what is called a "special interest". It's something that they really like and know a lot about. Often, people with AS can be so focused on their special interest that they ignore other things that are going on around them.

Mark's special interest is buses, but anything can become a special interest to someone with AS.

Sometimes a person's special interest will change from one thing to another. Having a special interest to focus on can make people with AS feel relaxed.

Special interests are usually things that are safe and stay the same – they're predictable. Knowing a lot about a topic gives a person with AS the feeling of being in control of things.

This can be important when the world around them seems very unpredictable and out of their control.

We're all interested in things, but people with AS may not understand that other people are not as interested as they are in their special interest.

Here we go again! Give it a rest, Mark – a bus is a bus...

People with AS can sometimes talk about their special interest <u>too</u> much for other people. They may find the person with AS boring, or think they seem obsessed.

33

As we follow the story of Sophie, Mark and the family, we'll see how and why it's important to understand these four main areas of Asperger Syndrome, and we'll see why it's important to understand special interests.

STRESS

We'll see that it's also important to understand stress, and how this can affect people with Asperger Syndrome and those around them.

Stress is the feeling you get when you are not sure what to do or what is happening. It's also the feeling you get when you think that things are "too much" for you to handle.

We all feel stressed at times, but some peole feel it more often. When people with AS get stressed, it can make their difficulties, differences and talents become more <u>extreme</u>.

You can think of stress like water being poured into a glass.

With each thing that happens to make you stressed – something going wrong, someone making you upset – a bit <u>more</u> water is poured into the glass.

Eventually, there's no more room in the glass and the water spills out everywhere.

When stress builds up inside us, it can "spill out" as us being angry or upset.

We'll be looking at ways in which stress affects Mark and the rest of his family – and at some ideas for dealing with stress.

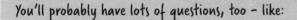

You know, it can be really hard when you find out that someone in your family has Asperger Syndrome. You can see in the next chapter how hard it was for all of us when we realised my dad had AS.

You might feel frightened or embarrassed – like I did.

You'll probably have lots of questions, too – like:

How will we cope?
What can we do?
Who can we ask for help?

Finding out about Asperger Syndrome and understanding it is a really important first step. Books like this one, family support groups and AS organisations, information from doctors, the library and the internet can all be helpful. In the next chapter, you can see how my mum found good information about AS and how it helped our whole family.

But although it <u>can</u> be difficult – even frightening – the <u>best</u> way to understand AS is for everyone in your family to talk about it.

Understanding Asperger Syndrome and how it can affect your parent is important. The more you understand, the easier you'll find it to cope with the everyday things that happen to you and your family.

In the next chapter, everyone gets very upset because of the way things happen at the Parents' Evening at Sophie's school.

But, as we'll explain, with a bit of understanding everyone can talk about how to start making things work better.

3. The Parents' Evening

We had a Parents' Evening at school and it was <u>AWFUL</u>.

It was Friday and that's the day that Dad works late. Mum booked us to see Ms. Farmer at 5:30, so Dad came straight to the school from work.

Parents get ten-minute slots with the teacher so that she can tell them how you're doing and show them the work you've done. I wanted to show Dad all the drawings I've done for our castle project. Ms. Farmer said she really liked them.

In "My School Musical", when Kaylee has school work, her dad Brent helps her and says she has a "can-do attitude"...

Well, my dad wasn't like <u>that</u> at the Parents' Evening...

Thanks a lot for taking the time, Ms. Farmer...

No problem, Mr. Deluchi. keep up the great work, Tony!

He was just <u>different</u> – as usual.

We've been waiting since twenty-two minutes past Five –

we had an appointment at half-past five.

It really doesn't matter, Ms. Farmer...

Excuse me...!

Um...Mark...

It's now almost SIX O'CLOCK. What's the point of having a timetable if you don't stick to it?

MARk!

I'm really sorry about that – we do always get a little bit late at the end of the evening. I do apologise, but obviously things overrun by a few minutes. We've still got plenty of time though, so why don't you come in and we can have a look at Sophie's fantastic drawings?

Dad just barged in. Of course we were going to be a bit late with our meeting – Ms. Farmer had just been talking to Tony and his Dad, and everyone knows that Tony has trouble reading...

I could tell Ms. Farmer wasn't happy about what Dad was saying – and neither was Mum.

40

Ms. Farmer showed Mum all the drawings of castles and knights that I had done. I wanted Dad to look at them, but he just walked around the room trying out all the chairs.

And what's this, Sophie? Oh – a catapult! Wow!

Well, um, maybe we can look at Sophie's dinosaur work...

Mark? Mark – you really should come and look at these drawings.

Dad? Can I show you my dinosaur stuff?

Mark – leave the chair. You really should come and have a look at Sophie's work.

Dad? Can I show you the picture of the catapult I drew?

Mark!

I was <u>so</u> embarrassed.

I wanted to...I don't know.

Dad then walked right out of the classroom, straight past Emily and her parents, and didn't even stop to say hello.

Um, you might find this leaflet useful...

Doesn't he care that people will say: oh look, there's Sophie...

...and her <u>weird</u> dad.

I really like school, and I really like Ms. Farmer.

I really wanted Dad to like my castle drawings...

But all he did was say what was <u>wrong</u> with them!

And who cares about the stupid <u>chair</u>, anyway?

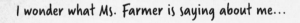

I wonder what Ms. Farmer is saying about me...

okay, Sam! Thanks for all your help!

Phew! Another Parents' Evening finished. Any problems with your lot, Liz?

There wasn't a problem, exactly – but, well, things with Sophie got a bit... awkward.

With Sophie? I don't understand? She's doing so well!

It wasn't her – it was her dad. I suppose you could say he was a bit... different.

Different? In what way?

He was very worried about the time – I mean, yes, I was running a bit late, but he got very agitated about it and made us finish promptly at six o'clock, even though we hadn't finished looking at Sophie's work – and Emily and her parents, who were next, would have been quite happy to wait.

Sophie's mum was very concerned about his behaviour, and I got the feeling from Sophie that this wasn't the first time her dad had behaved like this.

And then there was the business with the chair...

The...um, chair?

?

Yes – it's not really important, but it all reminded me of that training that we did last term – about AS. I wondered if Sophie's dad might have Asperger Syndrome.

His agitation about time, and not being able to focus on anything else – and the fact that he couldn't see how upset Sophie was...

47

I had some leaflets from the training session, so I gave one to Sophie's mum. As I said, it was all a bit awkward, but I told her to talk to us if she had any questions.

Yes, of course – that's great, Liz!

Don't worry, Liz – now that we know, maybe we can help Sophie – and her dad! I'm sure we can think of ways to make these meetings go more smoothly...

...for everyone!

I'll be happy to help Sophie – and her family!

49

Mark, <u>listen</u> to me. The way you treated Sophie and her teacher this evening was just plain <u>rude</u>.

The teacher was late. She should plan her meetings better. Now <u>we're</u> late with dinner –

Just forget the time thing for the moment, Mark. I'm talking about <u>Sophie</u>.

Sophie??

What has this got to do with <u>Sophie?</u>

You were <u>VERY</u> rude to Sophie, Mark! You hurt her <u>FEELINGS!</u> You did NOTHING but <u>CRITICISE</u> her drawings!

They were full of <u>mistakes</u>, Vicky. What she needs –

What she NEEDS is <u>encouragement</u> – NOT criticism! She's NINE! You can't talk to her like you did!

I was HELPING – something her teacher should be doing. I was <u>BEING INTERESTED</u>.

Okay, be interested in the things she likes, but don't be so CRITICAL. Sophie likes school – it's important that she feels happy there.

Well it's important to get spelling right, too.

Oh, MARK! Encourage her! Tell her she's doing well in school! Tell her that you're proud of her!

She knows I am...

She <u>won't</u> if you DON'T TELL HER, Mark!

I will... But we need to get a move on. We're already <u>late</u> for dinner.

oh for heaven's sake...!

No one talked during tea. Even Daniel could tell that something wasn't right.

Dad stayed very...quiet.

Mum made me and Daniel chicken bakes and green beans with smiley-face potatoes...

But I didn't feel like smiling...

I went upstairs to my room after tea and played with my sticker collection, but I wasn't really paying attention. It was all quiet downstairs for ages, and then I heard Mum say to Dad:

"Mark...we need to talk."

KAYLEE
BRETT
GO COUGARS!

Okay, why don't we look back over the Parents' Evening and try and figure out <u>what</u> happened – and <u>why</u>.

obviously, the big thing was that Mark was not happy when the appointment didn't start on time.

He told the teacher she was late, and needed to keep better track of the time...

He then said that everyone had to go exactly when the appointment was scheduled to end.

What's the big deal with not always being on time? And why did he have to be so mean to me – and so rude to Ms. Farmer?

Those are two really good questions, Sophie. Let's look at your first question, which is about <u>time</u>.

Remember some of the things we talked about in Chapter 2?

liking things to be the same   doing the same things

liking routines

lack of flexibility

things happening at the same time

taking longer to understand

knowing what is happening when

knowing in advance

schedules and timetables

one way

Sometimes people with Asperger Syndrome have difficulty managing time – particularly when things happen at the last minute, like when schedules or appointments get changed.

This is because they feel most comfortable if they know for certain <u>what</u> is going to happen <u>when</u>.

54

Dealing with last-minute changes to when things are supposed to happen takes flexibility and <u>imagination</u> – and some people with AS can find this difficult.

They find it hard to <u>imagine</u> things happening differently from the way they expect – and sometimes they don't know what to do if that happens.

And when Mark started to worry about the time, he started to worry about other things, too – things that maybe didn't seem important to everyone else...

Like the chair!

Like the chair, exactly.

It probably <u>was</u> too small, and maybe because he couldn't do anything about the time – about the meetings running late – he tried to solve the problem of the chair, instead.

People with AS also sometimes have difficulties with things to do with emotions and relationships...

...and communication. This means that people with AS can sometimes have difficulty understanding other people's feelings.

So when your dad said those things about your work, he said them without really understanding just how rude they might sound. Your mum might try to make the same kind of comments, but in a way that wouldn't hurt your feelings.

You've spelled "castle" wrong.

You've written "theyre" instead of "they're". You havent put a capital letter here.

What's this word, Sophie? Is it French? Oh – Welsh! Very clever, Sophie!

Let's have a spelling competition like they do in "My School Musical"!

So your dad certainly didn't <u>mean</u> to be rude, and he didn't <u>mean</u> to hurt your feelings...

But because he finds it difficult to understand other people's feelings, he didn't understand that the way he said those things would sound rude.

He also didn't <u>mean</u> to make you and your teacher feel unhappy and embarrassed.

But by the end of the day, everyone was feeling bad...

Why is everyone in such a bad mood?

I understand now – I know why Dad was so rude! He was worried about the time, and because of his AS he didn't understand that it was okay for the appointment to be late and take longer than we thought it would!

Time and being late for tea were the problems – not the chair, and not my spelling! So if time and being late were the problem, then... then maybe we could figure out some way to not be so late?

That's great, Sophie! Now that you understand a bit more about how AS works, you can think of ways to work around – or with – some of your dad's AS difficulties, differences and talents. You've got some ideas to help Sophie out, don't you, Kirsti?

I do, John. Any situation to do with time can become stressful – not just the "Parents' Evening" kind of appointment we've been talking about in this chapter.

So here are some suggestions that might help...

1. Perhaps Mark could have arranged to leave work early so that they could have a slot near the <u>start</u> of the Parents' Evening.

2. Maybe explain to Ms. Farmer before the day of the meeting that Mark likes to keep to time. She could then reassure him beforehand that it's okay for the appointment to last more than ten minutes.

3. Mark, Vicky and Sophie could talk to all Sophie's teachers. Once they understand, They might be able to help find a better time to meet.

4. Sophie and Vicky can help Mark by telling him clearly if he's making people feel uncomfortable, angry or hurt – but they must remember that <u>he</u> might be feeling angry or confused himself.

1. If there's a choice of times for an appointment, try picking an early one – there are less likely to be delays.

2. Make sure everyone involved in the appointment understands in advance if scheduled events might end up being shorter or longer.

3. Avoid sudden or last-minute changes to plans if possible. Perhaps have a "Plan B" and reschedule the appointment in advance if it looks like last-minute change is going to be unavoidable.

4. Talk about feelings often. Explain clearly what makes people feel angry, sad, hurt or embarrassed – and why these feelings are important to people. Talk about how different people might have different feelings from each other.

It wasn't <u>just</u> time and being late that made the Parents' Evening so difficult for Mark.

Changing Mark's routine — having to come to school after work instead of going straight home like he usually does — might have made him feel uncomfortable.

And Mark might have been anxious about going into Sophie's school. He might not have very good memories of when he was at school - many grown-ups with Asperger Syndrome don't. The school might also not be a place he knows very well, and he might not have met Ms. Farmer before. Sometimes, dealing with new places and new people can make people with AS very worried - and <u>stressed</u>.

We talked a bit about stress in Chapter 2 - and we'll look at it again more closely in the next two chapters.

I think everyone's learned something today...

I've learned that things to do with time – like appointments and last-minute changes – can be difficult for people with AS, like my dad. But I've also learned that there are things my whole family can do that can help make these situations easier for us to deal with.

And we've learned that it's important to explain AS to everyone. Teachers like us can help because there may be things we can do to help make appointments go more smoothly for everyone – Mark, Sophie, his family and us.

And what has Vicky learned...?

It can be hard finding out someone in your family has Asperger Syndrome. It can be frightening and confusing, and you may end up with more questions than answers at first.

That's why it's important to get good information and good advice. Vicky got some good information from the leaflet Ms. Farmer gave her at school, and you can find more good information on the internet.

But <u>watch out!</u> There can find a lot of misleading and out-of-date information about Asperger Syndrome and Autism online.

Talking to professionals – like teachers – is a great way to find out <u>good</u> places to learn online. And we've also listed some nationally recognised organisations and helpful online resources in the <u>Online safety</u> section at the end of this book.

65

4. The holiday

HAVEN PARCS

I can't wait! I had such a
great time last summer.

There are loads of things to do...

The beach, the play club, the
sand activity area - everything!

It's the <u>BEST</u> place for a holiday <u>EVER</u>!

HAVEN PARC
FAMILY ACTIVITY   HOLIDAY VIL

BEACH
AND FUN CLUB

ACTIVITY
PAVILLION

I'm <u>SO GLAD</u> we're going back!

We went there last year – all of us: me, Daniel, Mum, Dad, Uncle Jase, Auntie Louise, Grandpa Fred, Lilly, Barney <u>and</u> their dog Buster!

It was so cool! We all stayed in the same chalet – and did <u>everything</u> together!

It was great!

We were right next to the beach and the activity club, so I got to do loads and loads of stuff.

I even got to go bike riding in the forest zone, and play in the big climbing zone in the activity club!

Everyone had a great time...

...well, everyone except Dad, maybe.

Dad always seemed to be in a bad mood with Louise, Lilly and Barney

　　　- and Buster.

Okay, I suppose they all did make a lot of noise - and mess...

And things kept, well...

　　...happening.

When I think about it, I suppose Dad did end up shouting at Louise a lot...

...which is exactly what happened on Friday, too...

Dad ended up shouting again...

...but this time, a <u>lot</u> more.

75

Everyone was really, <u>really</u> happy about the baby - but not Dad...

He started shouting and shouting. He shouted at Louise, saying really mean things -

That the baby would cry and ruin our holiday, just like Barney had ruined last year's holiday. He said that Louise was stupid and selfish for having another baby when she couldn't manage the ones she already had...

He got more and more angry...

Mum was really upset. She tried to get Dad to calm down, but he wouldn't listen. He just <u>kept shouting</u>.

It was horrible.

He shouted at Lilly and Barney...

...and started fighting with Uncle Jase...

...and kicked Buster.

Uncle Jason told Dad he was right out of order, and Grandpa Fred told Jason to calm down and Jason told him to keep well out of it. Buster was howling. Lilly and Barney were screaming...

...and Louise started to cry and cry...

Mum, Grandpa, Jason and Louise went into the kitchen and argued about Dad...

I heard Mum say, "You know what he's like..."

And Dad?

He went into the front room and organised his bus models...

He stayed there all evening and was totally quiet...

...as if nothing had happened.

Poor Sophie! Poor everyone! This should have been a great evening. The whole family were getting together to discuss their summer holiday plans...

They'd planned the evening in advance. The whole house was full of people, and everyone was pleased to see each other...

Louise even had a great surprise to tell the family!

So what happened?

Why, when everyone was so happy, did Mark get so angry?

Why, when they'd worked hard to plan things in advance, did Mark behave like he did at the Parents' Evening?

Well, let's start by thinking back to what we talked about in Chapter 2...

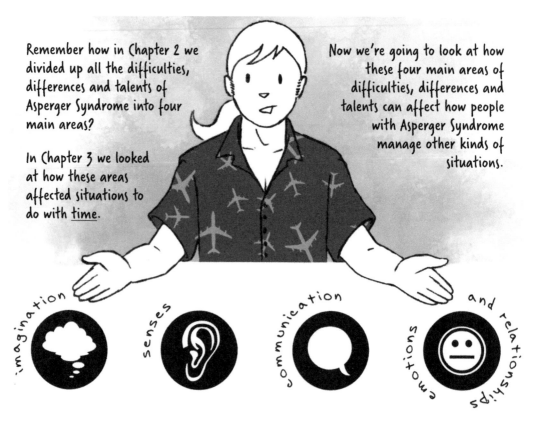

Remember how in Chapter 2 we divided up all the difficulties, differences and talents of Asperger Syndrome into four main areas?

In Chapter 3 we looked at how these areas affected situations to do with <u>time</u>.

Now we're going to look at how these four main areas of difficulties, differences and talents can affect how people with Asperger Syndrome manage other kinds of situations.

imagination

senses

communication

emotions and relationships

Let's start with <u>senses</u>. Senses are important because we use them to tell us what's going on around us. Sometimes, people with AS can find that if there's a lot of information coming to one of their senses, it can be difficult to focus on what's important.

In a noisy room, for example, where there are lots of people talking, it can be difficult for someone with Asperger Syndrome to pay attention to a conversation.

And it was very noisy in the house on Friday, wasn't it?

Mark has particular difficulty with hearing. He doesn't find it easy to separate out the sound of a conversation from other noises and the sounds of other people talking.

So for him, all that sound simply becomes one big, confusing <u>NOISE</u>.

It can make him feel very <u>left out</u>.

And the more going on, the more left out he can feel – because, don't forget, hearing is only one of the senses that can be affected by AS.

Separating out other things can be difficult as well.

The house wasn't just full of sound – there was a lot more to see, too: there were more people than usual, plus two small children and a dog all moving around. Mark isn't used to that.

What do you think, Sophie? What other sense things might have made things difficult for your dad?

What do you think? What other sense things might cause difficulty for someone with Asperger Syndrome?

Let's have a look at things to do with <u>communication</u> and <u>imagination</u>, now. Mark was expecting everyone to be talking about the holiday – not about dumplings, cats or new babies.

Of course, everyone was going to talk about the holiday – but that didn't mean that they couldn't also talk about other things. But Mark clearly found this a bit difficult.

As can make it difficult for people to manage situations that are different from what they expected. We saw a bit of this in Chapter 3.

In this chapter, Mark found it difficult to cope when it seemed like everyone was going to talk about anything and everything except the summer holiday plans.

Getting ready for unexpected situations, being able to cope with plans that change suddenly and managing things that are different from how you expected them to be...

...these are all aspects of AS to do with <u>communication</u> and <u>imagination</u>.

After what happened at the Parents' Evening in Chapter 3, Vicky did a good job of thinking about how Mark's AS affects his ability to cope with unexpected changes to <u>when</u> things happen.

She made sure they picked a good time to talk about the holiday...

...and that everyone knew when that was going to be.

But, as we've seen, it's not just unexpected changes to <u>when</u> but also to <u>what</u> that can be difficult for some people with AS. All Week, Mark - like Sophie - was expecting an evening of talking about the holiday.

But Mark was expecting to talk <u>only</u> about the holiday...

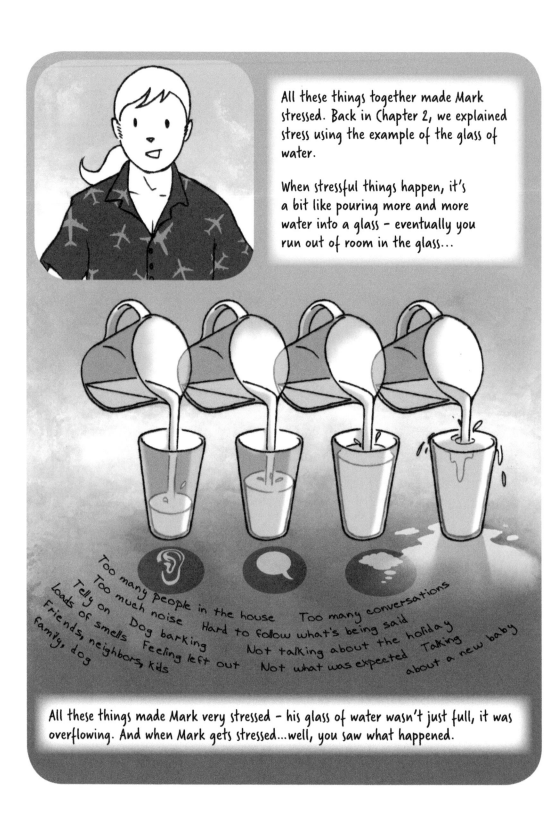

All these things together made Mark stressed. Back in Chapter 2, we explained stress using the example of the glass of water.

When stressful things happen, it's a bit like pouring more and more water into a glass - eventually you run out of room in the glass...

Too many people in the house   Too many conversations
Too much noise   Hard to follow what's being said
Telly on   Dog barking   Not talking about the holiday
Loads of smells   Feeling left out   Not what was expected   Talking
Friends, neighbors, kids   about a new baby
family, dog

All these things made Mark very stressed - his glass of water wasn't just full, it was overflowing. And when Mark gets stressed...well, you saw what happened.

But why did Mark shout at <u>Louise</u>? Why did he say that her new baby would ruin the upcoming summer holiday? Why did he blame Louise and Barney for ruining last year's holiday?

<u>Emotions and relationships</u> is another area where some people with AS can have difficulties. They find it difficult to understand how <u>other</u> people feel...

...and how what they say and do might affect people around them.

As a result, sometimes people with AS can behave in a way that seems very extreme – perhaps, like Mark, suddenly getting very, very angry without warning. Sometimes they can behave in a way that seems unreasonable or inappropriate, and end up being mean and rude. Remember how Mark acted at the Parents' Evening? When Mark gets stressed, he doesn't realise that the things he says and does can be hurtful and maybe even frightening.

All Mark could think about when he got stressed were his own bad memories of last year's holiday.

Now that we've had a look at what the problems were, let's look at some ways that might make a situation like that evening work better for Mark...and for everyone!

1. Try to make sure there's <u>not too much happening</u> at the same time. Turn off radios and televisions, for example, if it's important to hear and talk clearly. Keep the number of people down and maybe avoid cooking or serving food if there are important things that need to be discussed by everyone.

2. A really easy way to make sure everyone in a big group - like a family - knows what's happening when is to use a big wall calendar. Pick one with enough space on it to write down what's happening on what days. Hang it where everyone can see it - in the front hall or the kitchen, perhaps.

sun	mon	tue	wed	thur	fri	sat
	1	2	3	4	5	7
8	9	10	11	12	13	14
15	16	17	18	19	20	21
22	23	24	25	26	27	28
29	30	31				

3. And remember what we talked about in Chapter 3 about <u>time</u> - picking a good time, and talking about things taking longer than expected.

88

4. If you have agreed to talk to someone with AS about something – talk about just that, not about lots of other things as well. If there's a group of you, talk about what's important first, and then maybe talk about other – not so important – things afterwards. Maybe even say clearly that you're finished talking about one thing before you start talking about something else. This will help the person with AS focus and not get stressed.

5. Stress can make people with AS behave in ways that make others angry or upset. By making sure that situations don't become stressful, you can make it easier for everyone to get along – particularly when there's something important going on.

These are some things that Vicky and the family could try to make situations like these less stressful for Mark and better for everyone: family, friends and neighbours.

I've been talking to Mark. He and I decided that we need to work harder to make evenings like these better for him - and for everyone. We talked through the ideas and Mark was happy to try some of them out.

We're going to start with a big calendar on the wall in the kitchen. Mark thinks that will be really useful.

We're a big family, and it's not always possible to keep the house as calm and quiet as Mark would like.

I also want to change the way we organise our Friday evenings.

I'd like to think of ways for all of us to get to do the things we like to do -

- the way we like to do them. I think that's important for Sophie and Daniel - and for me.

And maybe we can find another chance to talk about the holiday...

In this chapter we've seen how difficulties with <u>communication</u>, <u>imagination</u> and <u>the senses</u> can make busy situations very stressful for people like Mark. We've also seen how stress and difficulties with <u>emotions and relationships</u> can lead to extreme or unreasonable behaviour.

But we've also seen how understanding why AS can make situations like these difficult is the first step to making things better. Vicky is thinking of using some of our suggestions to help come up with ways of helping Mark – and the whole family.

And we now know that to make it work for everyone, we all have to maybe plan a bit better. And that's exactly what we've all started to do...!

5. Making Time for Yourself

94

It was Lucy's idea – Spanish dancing reminds her of being on holiday!

We used to go to the classes whenever we felt like it – Monday, or Wednesday, or Friday...

But we now understand how difficult that can be for Mark. He used to get stressed because he didn't know <u>what</u> was happening <u>when</u>.

So now we do things <u>differently</u> – in a way that is better for Mark, yes, but in a way that is actually better for everyone...

We've found a way for everyone to get to do the things they like to do...

...in the way they like to do them!

This is what we do...

We have a schedule for the day, which we've all agreed on in advance. I get off work early and drop Daniel and Sophie off at 5:00 with Jase and Lou. They get to spend the night at their house...

Lucy comes round in the taxi at six o'clock.

BEEP!
BEEP!
BEEP!
BEEP!

Right, that's Lucy and the taxi – I'm off, Mark. Did you and your dad get something for tea?

Yes, of course. We're having pies and green beans at 6:15.

In the oven now, Vicky. Off you go – we'll see you at eleven!

Come on, Vicky! We haven't got all night! Ha, ha!

Go on, Mike – hit that horn again!

It's important for everyone in the family to get time to do what they like doing. It might be doing something <u>loud</u> and <u>exciting</u>, like playing video games or football, doing karaoke...

...or going out dancing!

Or it might be doing something quiet and calm, like having a long, relaxing bath, watching a favourite DVD or patiently building a model kit.

What's important is making some time for yourself...

Everyone in the family has had a chance to do the things they like to do, which gives everyone a chance to relax.

Relaxing helps us deal with <u>stress</u>. Remember: it's not just people with AS who get stressed – we <u>all</u> do!

Stress can make us unhappy, worried or angry.

When Mark feels stressed, he finds it difficult to focus on the important things.

But when he's not stressed – when he's had a chance to relax by doing something he likes – he can take the time he needs to process things at his own speed and focus on them properly –

things that are important for him... <u>and</u> the people around him.

It's really nice to see Vicky taking time to relax. She really needs it. I know that sometimes she gets tired and a bit down. Mark's a really nice guy, but sometimes he's...not easy to live with. I'm glad we've found a way she can get a break and we can both have a bit of a boogie!

Mark's not really one for going out, and I know Vicky likes to – so this works out well. I miss my quiz night every once in a while, but I don't mind – it's really nice to spend time just with Mark. What with the kids and the rest of the family, we don't get many chances.

Yeah, Mark winds me up sometimes. To be honest, I don't know how Vicky does it. But we love having the kids over. I know Jase gets on really well with Daniel, and Sophie's great with kids – having her around gets those monkeys of mine out of my hair for a while!

So I had a look online. There is a lot of information about Autism and AS.

I think it's best to start with "proper" websites – it can get a bit confusing otherwise...

There is so much information out there.

I'm also going to make an appointment to see our GP. I know I'm not ill, but it's a really good place to start.

A doctor will be able to help me find out if I need a formal diagnosis...

...and what support may be out there for us.

I'd also quite like to find out about groups where I can meet other people with AS...

...I think it could help me learn more about myself and how my AS makes me who I am.

I want to do this for the whole family - perhaps most of all for Sophie.

I want to do it so we can book the holiday for this summer. By then I'll have lots of ideas about how to make it work better for me with my AS...

...and for all of us!

oh Mark - those are great ideas! How thoughtful of you! I know Sophie will be <u>very</u> pleased!

I'll talk it over with Lou, Jase and your dad tomorrow...

6. What About Me?

I suppose that when we were little, me and Soph didn't really notice about Dad. But now that I think about it, yeah: he was different then, too. We had fun, doing stuff that Dad liked – but we were too young to really care that we _only_ ever did stuff Dad liked.

But I'm older now. I don't want us to just do the things Dad likes...I want us todo things that I like, too.

I remember when I was little, it didn't seem like such a big deal. He sometimes used to come and watch me play when I was on the "Bee Team"...

Thinking about it, I realise he didn't like it. Back then, I didn't really notice...

...but I notice now.

It's <u>hard</u> having a parent with AS. There are lots of things that can make you feel bad.

I used to feel angry that Dad didn't come to the park and watch me play football.

I thought he wasn't interested in me...

But think of all the people in the park...

All the noise...

Everything moving so quickly...

And the dogs!

I understand NOW why it could be <u>difficult</u> for Dad to like football – and I know it's <u>NOT</u> 'cause he doesn't like <u>ME</u>. I like football because I'm good at it, and that makes me feel good. So if I get a bit <u>down</u> about Dad and stuff, going to matches with Uncle Jason and kicking a ball around always makes me feel better.

If things get too much at home, it's good to have something <u>outside</u> the family that really interests you...

Something that you can do well and that makes you feel good.

Community centres, libraries and youth clubs all have activities that you can get involved in.

And if you think you need to talk about your feelings, then don't be embarrassed about finding someone you trust who you know will listen to you.

It could be a relative, a friend or a teacher at school. Talking is a great way of sorting out feelings and feeling better about them.

You could also write a diary...put down all the things that worry you, make you feel angry or get on your nerves...

I write about how I feel about Dad and his AS and everything in my diary!

Just like Sophie!

or chill out with some music...

...or just spend time with your mates.

You _can_ still do that and still think about other people as well.

Be clear about what you want, but remember:

We _all_ have feelings that can be hurt – even people with AS!

But you know what? I might think I want to do that – but I don't – not really.

I know it would just make Dad worried and upset, and that's just mean.

(Plus, I'll get grounded – again!)

So the only real option is to be honest, isn't it?

Yeah, I know – some of your friends might not think that's very cool. But you know what? If your friends are worth keeping, they'll understand. Trust me: they will.

Actually, the reason is because my dad has something called Asperger Syndrome – means he totally freaks out when things don't happen at the right time. That's why I've got to get home for five...

Huh. Well at least your dad cares when you come home...

You know – Ben's got a point: Dad does care – he cares where I am and he cares about what I'm doing.

That means a lot.

I guess I'm pretty lucky. And you know what else? It doesn't matter if Dad doesn't like football – I guess I don't like buses much!

So what if we're not the same? It's perfectly okay that we're DIFFERENT.

Anyway, I'm extra lucky because I've got Uncle Jason, too – who does like football. I'm going round to his tonight to watch Town F.C. bring home the League Cup, and –

Huh? What's going on at home?

121

123

I came straight from work!

Thank you Lucy! It's chaos here – and Mark...

CLUNK

Daniel! Turn that –

Wait...

What is that?

That's RMF9985 – the only original open top Routemaster in Town & County service –

But it's not in it's proper colours! What's going on?

Um, those are Town F.C. colours, Dad – they're bringing the cup home. First time since 1963.

Town & Country Bus Association restored that bus and used to give rides around the park road. We took you on it when you were little.

I've been on that bus? No way! That's so cool!

Mark? Lucy's here, and – DANIEL! Turn that off! You know your dad –

Eh?

Look, Vicky: it's Town F.C. bringing home the League cup. On RMF9985.

Everything's cool, Mum!

Say hi to Auntie Louise for us!

oh! Um... okay. I'll...see you later...

Daniel and his dad have found something they share an interest in! And it's helping them both during a difficult situation.

Okay, so Daniel's watching telly for the football and Mark's watching it for the bus – but they're still doing it together.

We've talked a lot about difficulties, but what about talents? These are things that someone with AS is particularly good at because they're different!

They come from aspects of AS that we've already talked about...

...like time and special interests...

The way that Mark thinks about time, his interest in detail – these are things that can be really helpful in difficult situations – these are talents! And now everyone in the family understands Mark's AS a bit better, they are learning to appreciate some of Mark's particular AS talents...

Organisation

Punctuality

Attention to Detail

Focus

It's easy to get down about AS and think that it's all just about difficulties and differences – things that all too easily become problems...

...both for the person with AS and for their friends, family and people they work with.

But the more you learn about AS, the more you understand that <u>talents</u> are an important part of what it means to be a person with Asperger Syndrome.

Appreciating Mark's AS talents is a way for Sophie, Daniel and the whole family to find more ways of spending time with Mark, and discovering things that might interest everyone.

All this is helping the whole family learn to understand each other better – and perhaps accept that they're <u>all</u> different!

7. Understanding Aspergers

Part of understanding AS is understanding that Asperger Syndrome isn't just about problems...

As they've all learned more about AS, Sophie, Daniel, their mum and I have started to see that AS brings talents as well.

We have all been learning more about AS and how it affects me and my family in _new_ ways.

Hullo, Mark! Come on in!

For example, I decided to go and see our GP...

Seeing a Doctor

You are **absolutely right**, Mark: AS is **not an illness** – but a formal diagnosis from me may be able to help you access certain kinds of help and services.

Most people think that you only go to the doctor if you're not well. But I thought that going to the doctor would be a good way for me to find out whether there was any other kind of support locally for people with AS.

Not everyone who has AS needs or wants to go to the Doctor. There are lots and lots of people out there with AS who don't need a doctor to tell them they have Asperger Syndrome or give them a formal diagnosis. But for me, I thought it would be helpful to have that recognition.

Having a diagnosis could help you get extra support at work, for example.

I'm going for my break now, Dave – it's 12:15.

Okay, Mark. I've done your list of jobs for this afternoon.

It has helped my employer and my workmates understand me and my AS – and how I work best.

Support Groups

And through my doctor, I'm now in touch with a local support group.

I've met other people with AS at the group. It's been good to meet them because they understand a lot of my experiences and feelings.

So, let's go round the group and each say what we've been doing since we last met.

We're all different, of course...

We'll all get two minutes. Mark — do you want to start?

...but we do have lots of things in common.

The group meets once every month. It's a good way to practise "being social" together. Not everyone wants to meet like this though – it can be a bit stressful. But nowadays, there's another way for groups like ours to "be social" –

133

- on the internet.

Social Media

Finding a safe and supportive online place to meet can be a brilliant way of communicating with others –

– without the stresses of face-to-face meetings.

There's advice on how to keep yourself safe online and suggestions for good websites to visit in the Online Safety chapter at the end of this book.

It sounds like you and the family have found lots of new ways to learn about AS...

What things have you found most useful?

Well, I've made a list...

I'm learning to "use" my special interest in buses to help me deal with stress.

My special interest helps me feel happy, calm and relaxed. Reminding myself that I can spend time with my models later helps me get through stressful situations.

Sometimes I even carry a vintage bus rally leaflet to help remind me.

I also realise that not everyone is as interested in buses as I am. Sometimes it can be hard for me to stop talking about buses once I've started, but Sophie and I have been practising some new rules with an egg-timer...

There were many detail ...ences in specification fro... ...London requirements s... ...on-opening windscreen... ...entilators, fluorescent in... ...heir own pattern of seat... ...ly, they had Leyland eng... ...rol semi-automatic gearbo... ...utomatic setting and... ...rear axle as... ...sual spiral...

okay, Dad – you've had your two minutes – my turn!

Today, Lacey and I watched the ... preview for the "My School ... series! It was awesome! Stevie ... that she was in love with Dexter ... in lo... ...so Stevie wa... and ... ...about ... bing ... Ma...

It's good for me to practise taking turns in conversations and listening to other people, even when what they are talking about isn't really very interesting to me.

135

We all know that certain things I find hard to cope with can easily upset me – and lead to a "meltdown".

2. UNDERSTANDING TRIGGERS

KNOWING WHAT CAUSES A MELTDOWN

JOIN IN FOR A WHILE

PLAN TIME APART, TIME ALONE

Hectic social situations – like when everyone came to our house to plan the holiday – are just too much for me.

Now we know this, we can work around it. It doesn't mean that we can't all still get together as a family. It just means that I'll join in for a while...

...and then I'll excuse myself and go off to my buses while everyone else continues. This works for the whole family.

And when we go on holiday, Jason and Louise are going to have a separate chalet to us – that way the kids and the new baby can be as noisy as they like. I can go to the Haven Beach bus rally in the afternoons and we can all meet up afterwards.

I'm still learning about some things - like my sensory issues.

3. SENSORY ISSUES
4. FLEXIBILITY & COMPROMISE

I enjoy going to Star Burger because I like to know exactly how my food is going to look, smell and taste.

But I understand not everyone wants everything to always be the same.

So this is connected to something else I'm learning about...

Maybe once you've tried Mrs. Chang's dumplings, Dad, we could think about going to the Panda Palace restaurant!

...which is empathy. I'm trying to see things from other people's points of view...

Hmm... one thing at a time, Daniel.

...to help me try new things - like the Chinese food Daniel likes so much.

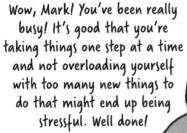

Wow, Mark! You've been really busy! It's good that you're taking things one step at a time and not overloading yourself with too many new things to do that might end up being stressful. Well done!

Hmm. Perhaps we could visit the family while they're on holiday and see how these ideas have helped them...

8. Being Different

It's been a full year for everyone. They've had to come to terms with Mark's AS and learn how to deal with his various difficulties, differences and talents.

They've done really well. They've learned how these things are divided up into four main areas...

...and how these affect the way someone like Mark deals with managing time, stress and situations that he can find confusing or difficult.

John and I have helped the family by showing them ways of dealing with AS in situations involving family members, teachers, friends...

oh, there you are...

Hey! Where did you get the ice cream?

It's all going _really_ well.

This summer has been _so_ much better than last summer.

Now that we all understand what works best for Mark, we can arrange things better. He's not stressed, I'm not stressed – and neither are Sophie and Daniel.

Of course, It's not perfect, and we're still learning new things. But that all just means we feel like a proper family again...

...a family that understands each other better.

I'm doing loads of stuff I want – like me and Jase playing in the Haven Parcs Family League!

This is a great holiday!

But because Dad gets to spend time watching the bus rally, too, it means that when we get together he's not stressed.

And when we get back to the chalet, I don't mind being quiet and just relaxing. After all that footie, I'm too tired to run around the chalet like I did last year!

Yes, this has been a better holiday. Things are better planned and I know what's going on.

I don't mind being on the beach with everyone – I can listen to my mp3 player and read behind the windbreak.

And the way we've organised our time means I get to spend my afternoons at the bus rally.

I still don't really understand why people think I'm different. The way I behave makes sense to me. But because I understand about Asperger Syndrome now, I know how it affects the people I love.

Everyone in the family has worked really hard to understand me and my AS. We've changed the way we do some things, and it's better for all of us, not just me.

It's not easy – it's not quick. But every day we understand AS a bit more, and figure out how to make things a bit better. I'm happier as a result – and I think...no, I <u>know</u> – everyone else is, too.

And speaking of everyone, there's rest of the family!

And who's that?

Is it...?

It's Louise and Jason's new baby!

Kirsti and John – say hello to Freddy!

It is!

We're really glad we've been able to help Sophie and her family – and we hope hearing about their story can help you.

Reading and thinking about some of the things we've talked about in this book might help you get on better with your AS parent, too.

We'll let the family enjoy the rest of their holiday…

And as this is her story, we'll leave the last word to Sophie…

I'm having a great time – this has been an amazing holiday!

Haven Parcs is just so cool! This year, I'm in the Junior Activity Club, which means I get to go on bike rides and do the rope course – and go on pony rides. And <u>Dad</u> said he'd go with me! <u>And</u> he found a place on Haven Beach where we can find real dinosaur fossils!

Did you know he likes horses? or fossils? No – neither did I!

But it's not just about all the cool stuff I'm getting to do – it's about more than that. Dad's so much happier this year – and it's because we all now understand about his AS. We've all learned new things and started to do things differently, and it's made us all happier.

I know my dad's <u>different</u> – but I also know this is what makes him <u>special</u>. What I've learned from all this is that if you understand why someone is different, it's easier to enjoy the time you spend together.

Well, it's almost tea-time, but <u>guess what</u>? Instead of eating here, Dad's suggested we go and get <u>chips</u> on the <u>pier</u>!

Mum asked him if he was sure about that, and he said <u>yes, of course</u> –

– he thought it would be nice to do
something different!

Sophie ♥

Afterword

In 2011, when we all first started finding out about Asperger Syndrome, John and Kirsti decided to tell our story as a comic book. They both felt that this was a really good way to show and explain things to younger readers, because sometimes pictures can make things easier to understand.

2011 was ages ago! Look how much we've all changed!

Sophie 2016

Kirsti 2016

Now, loads more artists and writers are making comics about health, medicine and wellness.

Comics allows people to present their own stories about their lives and experiences about living with illnesses, disabilities or conditions like Asperger Syndrome.

John 2016

Comics can be used to present information about all sorts of subjects.

In addition to making comics about medicine and health, I also make comics about archaeology and science.

And I'm finding out more about Autism and Asperger Syndrome in girls and women. We're all beginning to realise that Aspergers isn't just a "man thing".

And John and I would like to do a comic book about it!

Comics might be a great way for you to tell a story you think other people would want to hear about your own experiences.

If you're interested in the idea of making comics about medicine, health and wellness, check out www.graphicmedicine.org for more information.

online Safety

phone   tablet   laptop

Mark and Vicky made use of the Internet to find out about Autism and Asperger Syndrome. Mark also goes online to use social media and talk to other people with Aspergers. The internet is an amazing resource for everything and anything these days, and there is a wealth of information out there. However, it's really important to remember to stay safe when you're using the internet. Here are a few suggestions for how to be safe online.

⭐ Think before you type! It can be easy to get drawn into arguments online. Of course, everyone is entitled to their opinion, but never make personal or rude comments about people.

⭐ When you're using social media to chat with other people, never give out details about yourself – such as where you live and where you go to school.

⭐ Many people meet up in the "real world" after getting to know each other a bit online. If you do arrange to meet someone, meet in a public place and always let someone know where you are and what you are doing.

⭐ If you start to feel uncomfortable about the way another person is talking to you online, tell someone - like your mum or dad or a teacher.

⭐ Finally, don't believe everything you see online.

And here are some good, safe websites about Autism and Asperger Syndrome:

- The National Autistic Society: www.autism.org.uk (United Kingdom)
- Autism Spectrum Australia: www.autismspectrum.org.au (Australia)
- Autism Canada: www.autismcanada.org (Canada)
- Autism Society USA: www.autism-society.org (United States)

Glossary

Unfamiliar words you may find both in this book and on various websites, leaflets, etc.

Agitated: feeling upset, nervous or angry.

Anxious, anxiety: feeling worried and scared.

Apologise: say sorry.

Apparent: what you can see.

Asperger Syndrome: Asperger Syndrome is an Autism Spectrum Condition. A syndrome is a collection of certain differences and difficulties. This one is named after Hans Asperger, a Hungarian doctor who lived from 1906 until 1980. He was the first person to see this collection of differences and difficulties in the children he worked with.

Awkward: difficult, uncomfortable.

Certain: sure, particular.

Comfortable: feeling okay, relaxed, not worried. **Uncomfortable** is the opposite of this.

Communicate, communication: talking and listening, reading and writing – any way of giving and getting information.

Compromise: meet halfway, give and take.

Criticise, criticism: say negative and unhelpful things to and about someone or something.

DSM-V: This stands for **D**iagnostic and **S**tatistical **M**anual of Mental Disorders. The **V** is the Roman numeral for the number five, as this is the fifth edition of this manual. It is an American publication and generally used as the definitive tool for assessment and diagnosis of conditions like Asperger Syndrome (*see also* ICD).

Diagnosis: when a doctor or other expert recognises a condition like Asperger Syndrome by looking at all of the difficulties, differences and talents a person has. Some people may benefit from diagnosis by a doctor as it may help them get extra support at work, college or school. A diagnosis may also help family members, work-mates and friends better understand and accept the behaviour of someone with Asperger Syndrome.

Embarrassed: a feeling of shame and discomfort.

Emotion, emotions: feelings, like happiness, sadness, anger, fear, worry, etc.

Empathy: understanding other people's emotions. Begin able to see things from another person's point of view.

Encourage, encouragement: say helpful, positive things to someone.

Expected: what you thought would happen, what you had planned. **Unexpected** is the opposite of this.

Extreme: a lot, an unusual amount of something.

Flexibility: being able to change plans and cope when things turn out differently.

Frustrated: feeling angry and upset, usually because something is stopping you from doing or having what you want.

Imagine, imagination: how our brains think about things.

In advance: before something happens.

Inconsiderate: not thinking about other people's needs or feelings. **Considerate** is the opposite of this.

Meltdown: when a person gets extremely agitated. Some people may scream, shout, hit out, run and hide, "shut down" or do something that makes them feel safer – like stimming (*see* Stimming).

Organise: put in order, sort.

Particularly: especially, even more.

Patient, patiently: being able to wait for something, or do something that takes a long time.

Process: to think about something and understand what it means.

Reasonable: fair, sensible.

Reassure: remind someone to feel that things are okay.

Routine: a set way or order of doing something.

Schedule: a plan or timetable. To **reschedule** is to change your plan, or to decide to do something at a different time.

Self-awareness: learning to recognise your feelings and behaviour.

Senses, sensory: things to do with hearing, seeing, smelling, tasting, touching, plus feelings of balance and space.

Stimming: shortened from the phrase "self-stimulation". A behaviour that makes a person feel better, often used during stressful situations, and often repetitive. Reciting favourite songs, phrases, lists of information or moving about are all forms of stimming.

Strategy: a planned way of doing something or coping with situations.

Stress: a feeling of anxiety, worry and fear.

Suggest, suggestion: giving someone an idea, or something to try.

Taking things literally: this is about not understanding that things people say sometimes mean something else. Like when someone says: *it's raining cats and dogs.* This means that it's raining a lot, not that animals are falling out of the sky!

Trigger: a particular situation or experience that causes upset or agitation.